CONTENTS

SCOOBY-DOO! AND YOU

3 SOLVE-IT-YOURSELF MYSTERIES
VOLUME 2

JAMES GELSEY & TRACY WEST

PUFFIN BOOKS

Published by the Penguin Group
Penguin Books Ltd, 80 Strand, London WC2R 0RL, England
Penguin Group (USA) Inc., 375 Hudson Street, New York, New York 10014, USA
Penguin Group (Canada), 90 Eglinton Avenue East, Suite 700, Toronto, Ontario, Canada M4P 2Y3
(a division of Pearson Penguin Canada Inc.)
Penguin Ireland, 25 St Stephen's Green, Dublin 2, Ireland (a division of Penguin Books Ltd)
Penguin Group (Australia), 250 Camberwell Road, Camberwell, Victoria 3124, Australia
(a division of Pearson Australia Group Pty Ltd)
Penguin Books India Pvt Ltd, 11 Community Centre, Panchsheel Park, New Delhi – 110 017, India
Penguin Group (NZ), 67 Apollo Drive, Rosedale, North Shore 0632, New Zealand
(a division of Pearson New Zealand Ltd)
Penguin Books (South Africa) (Pty) Ltd, 24 Sturdee Avenue, Rosebank, Johannesburg 2196, South Africa

Penguin Books Ltd, Registered Offices: 80 Strand, London WC2R 0RL, England

penguin.com

The Case of the Bigfoot Beast
First published in the USA by Scholastic Inc., 2000
Copyright © 2000 by Hanna-Barbera
The Case of the Glowing Alien
First published in the USA by Scholastic Inc., 2000
Copyright © 2000 by Hanna-Barbera
The Case of the Seaweed Monster
First published in the USA by Scholastic Inc., 2001
Copyright © 2001 by Hanna-Barbera

This collection first published in Puffin Books 2007 ·
1

Copyright © 2000, 2001, 2007 Hanna-Barbera
SCOOBY-DOO and all related characters and elements are
trademarks of and © Hanna-Barbera (s07)

Typeset by Palimpsest Book Production Limited, Grangemouth, Stirlingshire
Made and printed in England by Clays Ltd, St Ives plc

British Library Cataloguing in Publication Data
A CIP catalogue record for this book is available from the British Library

ISBN: 978-0-141-32224-7

THE CASE OF
THE BIGFOOT BEAST

"Glad you could make it," Daphne calls to you as you walk into the diner.

Servers carry plates of food to the booths in the busy place. Daphne, Fred, Velma, Shaggy, and Scooby-Doo are seated by the window. You join them.

Daphne slides over and makes room for you in the booth. You sit down. Across the table, Shaggy and Scooby are steadily munching on a foot-high stack of pancakes.

"Like, this is so much yummier than that back-to-nature food we've been eating at the campground," Shaggy says. "Nothing but nuts and berries. Right, Scoob?"

Scooby slurps up the pancakes in one

bite. He nods his head. "*Ruts and rerries. Ruck!*" Scooby makes a face.

"We went on a camping trip," Fred explains. "There's nothing like a little fresh air to clear your mind after solving a mystery."

"Of course, we found *another* mystery at the campground," Velma says. "We just can't seem to escape them."

"We didn't just find a mystery. We found a monster, too," Shaggy says, shivering. "Man, that thing was big and hairy!"

Velma looks at you. "We sure could have used your help."

"You like solving mysteries, don't you?" Daphne asks. "We call this mystery *The Case of the Bigfoot Beast*," she says. "Why don't you read our Clue Keeper?" she asks as she hands you a colorful notebook. "You can try and figure out the mystery as you read. I was the writer for this mystery's entries."

"We write down the details of the mystery in the journal," Fred says. "The people we meet. The clues we find. They're all in there."

"We've even made them easy to find," Daphne continues. "When you see these spooky eyes , it means we found a suspect. And a means we found a clue."

"At the end of each entry, we'll help you organize the information you've found," Velma added. "All you need is a pen or pencil and your own Clue Keeper notebook."

You take the Clue Keeper, a little nervous. Are you really as clever at solving mysteries as the Scooby Gang?

Fred smiles at you. "Don't worry. I bet you'll crack the case in no time!"

Clue Keeper Entry 1

"Like, are we there yet, Daphne?" Shaggy asked, huffing and puffing. He had a heavy duffel bag on his back.

"Almost, I think," I answered.

Fred had parked the Mystery Machine in the parking lot of the Happy Camper Camp-ground. Then the gang and I had started hiking up the hill to the camp-ground entrance.

"I think that's the office up there," Fred said. He pointed to a small log cabin.

A man with a white beard stood in front

of the cabin. He was talking to a tall, bald man wearing a suit.

"You're making a big mistake, Walden!" said the bald man. "I'll make you an offer you can't refuse."

He stormed off down the other side of the hill. The bearded man shook his fist.

"I'll never sell!" he cried. "Never!"

"He sure looks like one *un*happy camper to me!" Shaggy remarked.

The man with the white beard noticed us. He smiled and held out his hand.

"Hello, campers!" he said. "I'm Henry Walden. Welcome!"

"Is everything okay, Mr. Walden?" Velma asked.

Walden's smile faded."Oh, you mean my argument with Rick Richardson," he said. "He's the owner of the resort down the hill. For years he's been trying to buy the campground from me so he can expand. But I love this place too much."

"I can see why," said Fred looking at the surroundings. "Where can we pitch our tents?"

Walden stroked his beard. "We've got lots

of campsites open," he said. "Follow me."

Walden headed down a path lined with tall trees.

"There's something creepy about this campground," Shaggy said.

Mr. Walden stopped. "Why do you say that?" he asked nervously.

Shaggy held out his arm. "Like, I've got goosebumps on my goosebumps," he said. "Everyone knows that woods are filled with spooks and ghouls and stuff."

"I hope you're wrong about that," Mr. Walden said as he continued down the path. The path led to a clearing.

"I'll help you set up camp here," he said. "It's a nice spot. It's near all the major trails." He pointed to three different trails leading into the woods.

Velma and I set up a small tent. Mr. Walden helped Fred set up another one.

"Shaggy and Scooby, you can sleep in here with me," Fred told them. "Do you want to unroll your sleeping bags now, guys?"

Shaggy and Scooby looked at each other.

"*Reeping rags?*" Scooby asked.

"You mean you didn't bring any?" Velma asked. "What's in that heavy bag?"

"Important camping supplies," Shaggy said. He opened his duffel bag. A tower of food spilled onto the grass.

Shaggy turned to Velma and me. "This is all Scoob and I need to survive in the great outdoors. As long as our stomachs are happy, we'll be happy. Right, Scoob?"

Shaggy turned back. Scooby-Doo was standing in front of the bag, which was now empty. He licked his lips with satisfaction.

Shaggy grabbed the bag and shook out the crumbs. "Like, this is terrible! We'll starve in these woods without food. We've got to leave right now."

"Please stay," said Mr. Walden. "You're my only campers this weekend."

"I was wondering about that," Velma said. "Why is the campground empty? It's the height of camping season. And why did you get so jumpy when Shaggy said the campground was creepy?"

Mr. Walden looked at his boots. Then he looked back at Velma. "I can't lie to you kids. Campers have been scared away from this place because of a story. A silly story."

"What story?" I asked.

Mr. Walden sighed. "People say the Bigfoot Beast is stalking the campground."

"*Rigfoot Reast!*" Scooby shrieked.

"I've never seen it myself," Mr. Walden said. "I assure you, this campground is safe. And I'm right down the road if you need me."

"Don't worry Mr. Walden," Fred said. "We've faced our share of monsters before. We'll be all right."

Mr. Walden nodded and headed back down the trail.

"I'm sure there's nothing to be worried about," I said. "We're going to have a great weekend, right guys?"

"Like, we'll have a good time as long as that Bigfoot Beast stays far away!" Shaggy replied.

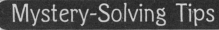

"Did you catch the  ? Fred and I thought you would. That means you've found the first suspect. Answer these questions about this suspect in your Clue Keeper notebook."

1. What is the suspect's name?

2. What kind of work does he do?

3. Why might he want to keep people away from the campground?

Clue Keeper Entry 2

It didn't take long for us to set up camp. Velma took a pair of binoculars out of her pack.

"I bet this is a great place for bird watching," she said. "Anybody want to come along?"

"Sounds like fun," I said.

"I think I'll work on getting us some dinner," Fred said.

"*Rinner?*" Scooby licked his lips.

"I think Scoob and I will stay with Fred," Shaggy said hungrily.

Velma nodded. "We'll be back soon."

Velma and I followed a trail. We marched along through the tall, dark trees. Soon the trees began to thin out, and we found ourselves in a clearing on top of the hill. Flat, gray rocks stretched out before us.

We walked onto one of the rocks and looked down at the scene below.

"Gosh," I said, "This sure is a nice view."

"Get off of there right now!" a voice cried.

We both spun around. A tall woman wearing jeans and a blue shirt was glaring at us. She wore a cap on her short, red hair. She carried a pack on her back.

"Those are Archaeotherium tracks you're stepping on!" the woman said angrily.

Velma and I looked down. Under my feet I could see what looked like hoof prints cut into the rock.

"We're sorry," Velma said, jumping off the rock. "The Archaeotherium is a prehistoric animal, right? You must be a paleontologist. A scientist who studies fossils."

"That's right," said the woman. "I'm Mindy Podwick."

Then she eyed Velma suspiciously. "You seem to know something about paleontology. Are you here to steal my discovery? Because I found it first!"

"Of course not," I replied. "We're here on a camping trip."

"We're just out bird-watching," Velma added. "We didn't mean to disturb you. Mr. Walden didn't mention anything about a fossil discovery."

Mindy Podwick's face clouded. "How many times do I have to tell Walden to keep people away from here? It's going to take me weeks to fully uncover these tracks. I'll never get my job done if heavy-footed tourists keep trampling the site."

Velma and I exchanged glances.

"We'll go bird watching somewhere else," Velma said. "Nice to meet you."

Mindy didn't reply. She was busy brushing dust away from the fossil prints.

"That was a little strange," I said as we walked away.

"You can say that again!" Velma agreed.

"Hey, did you spy the 👀 back there? You've found another suspect! Answer these questions in your Clue Keeper notebook."

1. What is the suspect's name?

2. What kind of work does she do?

3. Why might she want to keep people away from the campground?

16

Clue Keeper Entry 3

Back at the campsite, Shaggy and Scooby-Doo each held a fork and knife.

"So Freddy," Shaggy said. "Like, where's that dinner you were talking about?"

"*Rmmm. Rinner!*" Scooby echoed.

"I haven't caught it yet," Fred replied.

Shaggy and Scooby looked at one another, confused.

Fred dug in his pack and took out a pocket fishing pole and a small tackle box.

"One of the reasons we chose this campground is that there's a stream here that's perfect for fishing," Fred said. "If I'm lucky, I can catch us some fresh fish for supper."

"Fresh fish?" Shaggy asked. "Like, do you think there are any pizzas swimming around in that stream?"

Scooby rubbed his tummy. *"Rmmm. Rizza!"*

"I'm pretty sure there are only fish," Fred said. "Do you want to come?"

"Fishing's just not my bag," Shaggy said. "I'd rather get my food from a snack machine."

"Fine with me," Fred said. "But I don't think you'll find any snack machines in these woods!"

Fred took off down a trail. Shaggy and Scooby sat down on a fallen log.

Grrrrrrrrr! A rumbling sound filled the air.

"What was that?" Shaggy asked, alarmed. "Is it the Bigfoot Beast?"

Scooby smiled sheepishly and pointed to his stomach.

"I know how you're feeling, Scoob," Shaggy said. "I'm so hungry I could eat this log."

Just then, a delicious smell wafted into their campsite. Shaggy and Scooby sniffed the air.

"Are you thinking what I'm thinking, Scoob?" Shaggy asked.

Scooby-Doo nodded.

"Let's follow that smell!" Shaggy cried.

Shaggy and Scooby followed their noses down a trail — the same trail Fred had taken. Soon they saw the stream flowing nearby. Then the trail forked to the right.

They followed the delicious smell and took the fork. Just up ahead, a small cave was set into the side of a hill. A man had a campsite set up in front of the cave. He was sitting in an old lawn chair cooking hot dogs over a fire.

"Who's there?" the man called out as he heard Shaggy and Scooby approach.

"Like, we're just some hungry travelers searching for a good meal," Shaggy said.

The man eyed them suspiciously. "How did you find me?" he asked.

"We followed our noses, right Scoob?" Shaggy said.

"*Right!*" Scooby replied.

"If I give you some food, will you leave me alone?" the man asked.

Shaggy and Scooby nodded.

The man pointed to some hot dogs cook-

ing over hot coals. The hot dogs were attached end to end on one long string.

"Help yourself," he said. "Name's Skinny. Skinny Miller. I'm the caretaker of this campground."

Skinny Miller lived up to his name. He was thin, with short, gray hair and piercing blue eyes. He was as tall as Shaggy, but his feet looked small compared to Shaggy's big shoes.

Shaggy picked up one end of the hot dog string. Scooby picked up the other. They chomped on the hot dogs until they met in the middle.

"Fancy meeting you here, Scoob," Shaggy joked. He gulped down the last bite and

looked at Skinny. "So, you're the caretaker. Like, isn't it weird working out here in these spooky woods?"

"This job wouldn't be so bad if that penny-pinching Walden would pay me what I'm worth," Skinny said. "I do all the work around here, and he makes all the profit."

"So, like, why don't you just leave?" Shaggy asked.

Skinny's face clouded. "I could have made a fortune in my family's jewelry business. But my father was a bad businessman. He lost everything. So I'm stuck here. Besides, these woods don't scare me."

"So I guess that story about the Bigfoot Beast is a big lie," Shaggy said.

Skinny looked him right in the eyes.

"Oh no," he said. "I've seen the Bigfoot Beast. He haunts these woods every night!"

Shaggy and Scooby's Mystery-Solving Tips

"Like, did you see the 👀 in that last entry? Groovy. Jot down the answers to these questions in your Clue Keeper notebook while Scooby and I go look for a snack."

1. What is the suspect's name?

2. What kind of work does he do?

3. Does he have a reason to keep people away from the campground?

Clue Keeper Entry 4

Later that night, the gang and I were all sitting around the campfire toasting marshmallows. Fred, Velma, and I each had one marshmallow on a stick. Shaggy and Scooby's sticks were filled with marshmallows from top to bottom.

Shaggy told us how Skinny Miller could have made a fortune in the jewelry business, but he was stuck working at the campground instead. But that's not what worried Shaggy.

"I'm telling you, Skinny said he saw the Bigfoot Beast," Shaggy was saying between bites. "He said it haunts the woods at night."

"I bet he was just teasing you," Velma said. "I'm sure Mr. Walden's right, and the Bigfoot Beast is just a silly story. I wouldn't be surprised if Mindy Podwick made it up. She doesn't want anyone near her fossils."

Shaggy still looked worried. "I don't know. Skinny seemed pretty convincing to me, right, Scoob?"

"*Mmm mmm*," Scooby replied.

"What's that, Scoob?" Shaggy asked.

Scooby pointed to his mouth. "*Mmm mmm mmm.*"

"I think Scooby's had one marshmallow too many," Velma said. "His mouth is stuck!" She handed Scooby a water bottle.

Scooby took a sip. "*Rat's retter!*" Scooby said.

Feeling tired, I stood up and yawned. "I'm going to get some sleep," I said.

"Me, too," Velma said. She followed me inside our tent.

"You mean we're really going to stay here overnight?" Shaggy asked. "What if the Bigfoot Beast gets us?"

Fred put out the campfire. "Don't worry, guys.

Just get a good night's sleep. I bet you won't even think of the Bigfoot Beast in the morning."

Fred walked into the boys' tent and climbed into his sleeping bag. Shaggy and Scooby rushed in after him. Since they hadn't packed any sleeping bags, they tried to get comfortable on the hard ground.

Fred fell asleep right away. But Shaggy and Scooby tossed and turned. Scooby's tail smacked into Shaggy's face. Shaggy's feet jabbed into Scooby's back.

"Like, this is a hopeless cause," Shaggy said. "We're never going to get to sleep."

Scooby-Doo sighed.

"Hey," Shaggy said. "I bet Mr. Walden has some comfy beds in that log cabin of his. We should go there."

Scooby looked scared. "*Rout rhere?*" He pointed out into the dark night.

Shaggy reached into Fred's pack and

took out a flashlight. "We'll be okay, Scoob. Mr. Walden's cabin is right down the road and besides, I bet there's food in the fridge."

"*Rokay!*" Scooby said.

Shaggy and Scooby stepped out of the tent. Shaggy shone the light on a trail.

"I think it's this way," Shaggy said.

Shaggy and Scooby walked through the dark woods. The flashlight lit the way ahead.

On the side of the trail, two yellow eyes glowed in the darkness.

Scooby jumped into Shaggy's arms.

"Zoinks!" Shaggy cried. "It's the Bigfoot Beast!"

The yellow eyes got closer. Then a little raccoon ran in front of the light.

Scooby jumped down, looking embarrassed.

"Like, it was just a little critter," Shaggy said.

Shaggy and Scooby marched on.

"We should have reached the cabin by now," Shaggy said, a little worried.

The trail opened up into a clearing.

"Man, Scoob, it looks like we took the wrong trail," Shaggy said, chuckling nervously. "We'll have to go back."

Then Shaggy and Scooby noticed another pair of eyes gleaming in the darkness.

"It must be another raccoon," Shaggy said. He called out. "Hey, little fella! Are you looking for your friend?"

The eyes got closer.

"Here, little guy," Shaggy said.

Something jumped in front of the flashlight. But it wasn't a raccoon.

It was a tall creature, taller than Shaggy. The beast was covered with long brown fur. It had two big, hairy feet.

"Like, it's the Bigfoot Beast — for real!" Shaggy cried.

"*Aaaaaargh!*" The Bigfoot Beast roared and lunged after Shaggy and Scooby.

Shocked, Shaggy dropped the flashlight.

"Run for it, Scoob!" Shaggy yelled.

Shaggy and Scooby tore back down the trail. They ran to the campsite and crashed into Fred's tent.

"Everybody run!" Shaggy yelled. "The Bigfoot Beast is after us!"

Clue Keeper Entry 5

Fred's tent came crashing down. Shaggy and Scooby got tangled up in the fabric. Fred stepped out of the mess.

Velma and I ran out of our tent.

"Jinkies!" Velma cried. "What's going on?"

Shaggy and Scooby tried to get out of the tent. But the fabric covered their eyes. They hopped around, trying to get loose. Then they crashed into our tent. That tent collapsed, too.

Velma pulled the tent off them.

"What's this all about?" Velma asked, yawning.

"Like, there really is a monster in these woods!" Shaggy said. "The Bigfoot Beast. We saw him. He chased us down the trail."

Scooby put his paws out in front of him and growled like the beast.

Shaggy explained how he and Scobby had gone out to look for Mr. Walden's cabin when they found the beast in the clearing.

"I believe you," Velma said.

Two flashlights appeared in the darkness. Skinny Miller came down one trail. Mr. Walden came down another.

"My goodness!" Mr. Walden said. "Is everything all right?"

"It is now, Mr. Walden," Fred said. "But a few minutes ago, Shaggy and Scooby saw the Bigfoot Beast!"

"I told you," Skinny said. "He haunts these woods at night. I've seen him. He's got beady eyes as red as rubies."

"That's him all right!" Shaggy said.

Mr. Walden glared at Skinny. Then the worried look returned to his face.

"Are you sure?" Mr. Walden asked. "Maybe it was just a deer."

Shaggy and Scooby shook their heads. "Like, this was a big, hairy, beast! There was nothing *dear* about it."

"This is terrible," Mr. Walden said. "I can't let people camp here if there's a beast running lose. I'll have to close the campground."

"Don't worry, Mr. Walden," Velma said. "We'll help you solve this mystery. If we find out what's behind this beast, you can keep the campground open."

"You kids will really help me?" Mr. Walden asked gratefully.

"Sure," Fred said. "We'll start investigating in the morning."

"I wouldn't go looking for that beast if I were you," Skinny muttered. "It's dangerous."

"We've seen our share of monsters before," Velma told him. "We can handle it."

Mr. Walden looked at the mess in their campsite.

"Why don't you all sleep in my cabin tonight?" he suggested. "I've got extra beds."

"Now why didn't we think of that, eh, Scoob?" said Shaggy.

"Thanks, Mr. Walden," I said. We all followed Mr. Walden to his cabin, and soon we were sound asleep.

In the morning, we all headed back to the campsite. Fred started to pick up the tent poles.

"I'll get this straightened out," Fred said.

"I'll help," I offered.

Velma turned to Shaggy and Scooby. "Why don't you show me where you saw the beast?" she asked.

Shaggy looked around the campsite. There were three trails to choose from.

"Like, I'm not sure which trail we took," Shaggy said. "We ended up in some kind of clearing."

"That sounds like the trail Daphne and I took yesterday," Velma said.

I nodded in agreement.

"Follow me," Velma instructed to Shaggy and Scooby.

Shaggy and Scooby were a little nervous as they walked down the trail. They expected the Bigfoot Beast to crash through the trees at any minute.

Soon the trail opened into a clearing. Mindy Podwick was kneeling on a long, flat rock. She looked upset.

"Did you do this?" she asked Velma. "I told you and your friend to stay away from here!"

"What happened?" Velma asked.

"Somebody's been walking all over my Archaeotherium tracks," she said. "I can tell because there are footprints everywhere."

Velma examined the footprints.

"They're not very big," Velma remarked.
She turned to Shaggy and Scooby. "Shaggy,
these are too small to be yours. And there
are no paw prints, so they can't be Scooby's.
They must belong to the Bigfoot Beast."

"Like, for somebody named Bigfoot, he's
got really small feet," Shaggy said.

"Good point," Velma said. She turned to
Mindy Podwick. "Are you sure they aren't
your own footprints?"

"They're about the same size," Mindy
Podwick said. "But I would never trample all
over my fossils. I know better than that."

She eyed Velma. "What's this about, anyway? Is it that silly beast that Skinny Miller keeps talking about?"

"It sure is," Shaggy said. "That hairy horror attacked us last night."

Mindy Podwick raised an eyebrow. "Really? I thought old Skinny was making it up. I can't say I minded it, though. At least it kept people away from my fossils. Until now."

"Well, we'll leave you alone now," Velma said, taking the hint that Mindy Podwick didn't want them around anymore.

"Okay...bye," Mindy muttered distractedly.

Velma led Shaggy and Scooby back down the trail. Birds chirped in the trees.

"Like, these woods aren't so scary when it's sunny out," Shaggy said. "I can't believe we saw the Bigfoot Beast here last night."

Scooby shivered remembering the events of the night before.

"After seeing those small footprints, I don't think we have too much to worry about," Velma said.

"Did you see the ⊙━▶ back there? That's your first clue. Write down the clue in your Clue Keeper. Then answer these questions."

1. What clue did you find in this entry?

2. What does this clue tell you about the Bigfoot Beast?

3. Which of the suspects could have left this clue?

Clue Keeper Entry 6

Back at the campsite, Velma told Fred and I about what happened in the clearing.

"It sounds like someone is behind this Bigfoot Beast," Fred said.

"I'd rather be *behind* it than like, in front of it!" Shaggy said. "That's one scary monster."

"Besides Mindy Podwick, who would want to scare people away from the camp?" I asked.

Velma thought. "How about the man Mr. Walden was arguing with yesterday? Mr. Richardson, the resort owner? If Mr. Walden has to close the campground, Richardson could buy it from him."

"Good thinking," Fred said. "I also think we should talk to Skinny Miller. He seems to be the one who's spreading these stories about the Bigfoot Beast. And he doesn't like Mr. Walden much. Maybe he's in on it somehow."

"I'll go with you, Fred," I said.

"Scoob and I will go with Velma," Shaggy said. He rubbed his stomach. "I bet that resort has a five-star restaurant."

Velma, Shaggy, and Scooby-Doo headed to the resort. When they reached the bottom of the hill, a fancy gate opened into a sprawling green lawn. A white mansion lay at the end of the road. Next to it was a sparkling swimming pool.

Velma spotted Mr. Richardson by the pool. They approached him.

"Mr. Richardson, we're staying at Mr. Walden's campground," Velma said. "We were wondering if we could talk to you for a minute."

"Certainly," Mr. Richardson said. He led

them to a round, glass table. "Why don't you join me for a snack?"

"*A Rooby Rack?*" Scooby asked.

"Like, Scoob, I think there'll be some fancy resort food at this place. That's even better than a Scooby Snack," Shaggy said, licking his lips. He sat down and flagged a waiter. "We'll have two of everything on the menu, please."

"Nothing for me, thanks," Velma said. "Mr. Richardson, we were wondering about your interest in Mr. Walden's campground."

"Oh, that," Mr. Richardson said. "That Henry Walden can be so stubborn. I've offered him a great deal of money. He just won't sell. I need that land so I can expand this place."

"Do you want it badly enough to drive Mr. Walden out of business?" Velma asked.

"Goodness, no," Mr. Richardson said. "Henry and I have been friends since we were boys. I'm sure my money will convince him in time."

Mr. Richardson crossed his legs. Velma studied his shiny black shoes.

"Those are nice shoes, Mr. Richardson," Velma said. "Do you mind if I ask what size they are?"

Mr. Richardson laughed. "They're a size sixteen! Big feet run in my family."

Velma stood up. "Come on guys," she told Shaggy and Scooby. "I think we can go now."

The waiter sat a covered silver tray in front of them.

"In a minute, Velma," Shaggy said. "Scooby and I are just about to dig in."

Shaggy lifted the lid. He revealed a plate piled high with carrot sticks, celery sticks, and lettuce.

"Like, what kind of snack is this?" Shaggy asked.

"This is a health resort, young man," Mr. Richardson said. "We only serve raw fruits and vegetables here."

"Thanks, Mr. Richardson," Shaggy said. "But Scoob and I will pass on the rabbit chow."

As they walked back up the hill to the camp, Shaggy's stomach rumbled.

"Maybe we should go see if Skinny has any more hot dogs," Shaggy said. "I'm hungry!"

"*Re roo!*" Scooby agreed.

"I'm anxious to talk to Skinny Miller myself," Velma said. She walked ahead quickly.

Shaggy sank down on a rock. "We'll catch up with you in a minute, Velma," he said. "All this back-to-nature stuff is wearing me out."

Scooby sat down next to Shaggy.

Up ahead, the tree branches rustled.

"Velma, is that you?" Shaggy called out.

"Aaaaaargh!" The Bigfoot Beast crashed through the trees. He waved his hairy arms and stomped his feet.

"Zoinks!" Shaggy cried. He and Scooby tore up the trail at top speed. They crashed into Velma.

"Hang on, guys," Velma said. "What's wrong?"

"B-b-b-b," Shaggy stammered.

"The Bigfoot Beast?" Velma asked.

Scooby nodded.

"Let's check it out," Velma said. She walked back down the hill.

The Bigfoot Beast was nowhere in sight. But Velma saw something glittering on the ground.

She took out her magnifying glass and knelt down. Then she picked up something very tiny. A chip of a shiny blue stone.

"Jinkies," Velma said. "This looks like a sapphire."

"Fire? Where's the fire?" Shaggy asked.

"I said sapphire," Velma said. "It's a valuable gem."

"Way out," Shaggy said. "You mean gems grow on trees in these woods?"

Velma shook her head. "Actually, sapphires are usually found in stream beds or gravel pits."

She stood up.

"We've got to find Daphne and Fred!" she said.

"Did you see the ⚬—▸ ? Velma found another clue. Man, I wish Scooby and I had a pizza for every clue she's found! While we're dreaming of pizza, you can answer these questions in your Clue Keeper."

1. What clue did you find in this entry?

2. Where on the campground do you think the clue could have come from?

3. Does this clue give a new reason for someone to scare people away from the campground?

Clue Keeper Entry 7

While Velma, Shaggy, and Scooby-Doo hiked back up the hill, Fred and I were looking for Skinny Miller.

We found the stream and the cave next to Skinny's campsite. The campfire was out. His shabby lawn chair was empty. Fred called into the tent, but no one answered.

"I wonder where Mr. Miller is?" I asked. I put my hand on Mr. Miller's chair and noticed something odd.

"Fred, look at this," I said. I picked up a book from the seat of the chair. "It's a directory of gem dealers — people who buy and sell valuable stones. I wonder what Skinny's doing with this?"

"I'm not sure," Fred said. "Shaggy said he used to be in the jewelry business. Maybe he's trying to get back in."

"I wish we could ask him about it," I said.

"We'll have to see if Mr. Walden knows where to find him," Fred replied.

"It's too bad he's not around," I said, walking toward the stream. "It's so pretty here," I said, looking at the water.

I looked closer. "That's strange," I said. "The bottom of the stream bed looks kind of sparkly."

"What are you kids doing here?" an angry voice cried.

Fred and I spun around. Skinny Miller was coming out of the cave with a scowl on his face. His gray hair stuck out on top of his head.

"Sorry, Mr. Miller," Fred said. "We're trying to help Mr. Walden solve this Bigfoot Beast mystery."

"There's no mystery," Miller said. "The beast roams these woods. Just like I told your friends."

"Mr. Walden might have to close this campground," I said. "Then you'd be out of a job."

Mr. Miller shrugged. "I don't get paid near enough anyway. I'd survive."

"Aren't you afraid the beast will come after you?" Fred asked.

"Nope," Skinny said. "The beast won't bother me."

"Why not?" I asked.

"Because unlike you kids, I know how to keep my nose out of places where it doesn't belong!" Skinny replied.

Fred and I left Skinny's campsite and walked back to our camp. Velma, Shaggy and Scooby were there waiting for us.

We all exchanged stories. Velma told us about the meeting with Mr. Richardson, and the sapphire they found in the woods. Fred told them about the book of gem dealers that Skinny had.

"Are you thinking what I'm thinking?" Velma asked.

Fred nodded.

"It's time to set a trap for the Bigfoot Beast!"

"Daphne and I found an important clue in this entry. Make sure you answer all of the questions about it."

1. What clue did you find in this entry?

2. Who does the clue belong to?

3. How does this clue connect to the clue Velma found in the last entry?

50

Clue Keeper Entry 8

It didn't take the gang and I long to come up with a plan. To make it work, we needed Shaggy and Scooby to lure the Bigfoot Beast out of the woods.

Fred handed Shaggy his fishing pole.

"Like, do you expect us to fish for the monster?" Shaggy asked. "We're looking for the Bigfoot Beast, not the Bigfinned Flounder."

"We need to find an excuse for you and Scooby to go near the stream," Velma said. "If my hunch is right, the beast won't want you to go anywhere near there."

"Right," Fred said. He held up a fishing net. "When the beast comes after you, we'll be hiding in the trees with Mr. Walden. We'll trap the beast in this."

"What do you mean, when the beast comes after us?" Shaggy said. "What if it gets us and eats us for supper?"

Scooby didn't like that idea. He crawled into Velma's sleeping bag.

"Come on out, Scooby," I said. "We'll be right there to protect you."

"*Ruh-uh*," Scooby said.

"Would you do it for a Scooby Snack?" I asked.

"*Ruh-uh*," Scooby said.

"How about three Scooby Snacks," Daphne said, "and a big stack of pancakes when this trip is over?"

"*Rokay!*" Scooby said. He popped his head out of the sleeping bag.

It didn't take us long to set up the trap. Luckily, the woods were deserted. We didn't see Skinny Miller or Mindy Podwick anywhere.

Shaggy and Scooby-Doo sat down on the stream bank. Shaggy cast the fishing line into the water.

"Like, Scoob and I are sure having fun fishing in this stream," Shaggy said in a loud voice. He reeled in the line. "Hey, look, I caught something."

Sticking onto the end of the hook was a hunk of sparkling blue stone.

"Wow! Look at this!" Shaggy cried. "It's just like the one Velma found this morning."

"*Aaaaaaargh!*"

"Gee, Scoob," Shaggy said. "You sure sound excited."

Shaggy turned and looked at Scooby. But Scooby wasn't saying anything. Scooby had his back turned to the stream. He was pointing in front of him with a terrified look on his face.

Shaggy turned around. The Bigfoot Beast was standing right over them.

"*Aaaaargh!*" the beast roared. His beady red eyes glared at Shaggy and Scooby. He stomped his big, hairy feet.

"Let's get outta here, Scoob!" Shaggy yelled, dropping the fishing pole. They both stood up, but the ground underneath their feet was soft and slippery. With a splash, they both fell into the stream.

The Bigfoot Beast followed them into the stream. Shaggy and Scooby ran out, covered with water and mud. They tripped over their feet as they ran, falling into a pile of leaves.

Shaggy and Scooby ran into the woods. The Bigfoot Beast wasn't far behind.

Then suddenly, a net fell over Shaggy and Scooby.

"Gotcha!" a voice cried.

Fred and Mr. Walden jumped out from

behind a tree. Fred's face fell when he saw who was in the net.

"Shaggy and Scooby!" Fred said. "We thought you were the Bigfoot Beast! The mud and leaves make you look like a monster."

"Never mind that now," I said. "The real beast is getting away!"

The Bigfoot Beast was running down the trail, toward the cave near Skinny Miller's campsite.

"Don't worry," Velma said. She came running through the woods carrying the fishing pole.

Velma cast the fishing line. The line flew

through the air, and the hook caught in the Bigfoot Beast's fur. The beast stopped in his tracks.

Fred and I ran up to help Velma. Together, we reeled in the beast.

The creature roared as he was dragged backward along the trail. Shaggy and Scooby untangled themselves from the net. Mr. Walden joined the gang and me, and soon we had the Bigfoot Beast surrounded.

"Like, there's something fishy about this beast," Shaggy said.

"You can say that again," Velma said. She turned to Mr. Walden. "Would you like to see who's been trying to scare people away from your campground?"

"You bet I would!" Mr. Walden said. He grabbed a fistful of the Bigfoot Beast's hair and pulled off his fake head.

"**M**ore pancakes, please," Shaggy calls to the waitress.

You look up from reading the gang's Clue Keeper.

"That was quite a case, wasn't it?" Daphne says. "You've met the suspects. You've found the clues. Do you want to try to solve the mystery?"

You nod your head.

"I knew you could do it," Velma said. "Let us give you some advice before you start. Look at your list of suspects and clues and answer these questions."

"First, who had a reason to scare people away from the campground?" Fred asks.

"Second, which of the suspects could have left the clues that the Bigfoot Beast left?" Daphne asks.

"See if you can eliminate any of the suspects first," Velma says. "Whoever is left is probably the person pretending to be the Bigfoot Beast."

The waitress brings two new stacks of pancakes to the table. The stacks are so high that they cover Shaggy's and Scooby's faces.

"Why don't you try to solve the mystery while Scooby and Shaggy work on those pancakes?" Velma says.

"That won't take long!" Shaggy says.

"When you're done, we'll tell you who did it," Fred says.

"Zoinks! It's your last chance to guess who's behind the Bigfoot scare. When you're ready with your answer, turn the page to find out who did it!"

"It was Skinny Miller, the caretaker," Fred says.

"Our first clue was the footprints," Daphne says. "The fact that they were small meant that we were dealing with a real person in a costume, not a monster with giant feet."

"Mr. Richardson's feet were too big," Velma says. "And I believed Mindy Podwick when she said she wouldn't trample her fossils. She cared about them too much."

"That left Skinny Miller," Fred says.

"That left the question — why?" Velma

says. "We knew Skinny complained about not having any money. But closing the campground wouldn't help him."

"We started to figure it out when Velma found that sapphire," Daphne says. "Then I noticed something sparkling in the stream bed near Skinny's campsite. And we found Skinny's book of gem dealers."

"We knew that Skinny knew something about gems and jewels," Velma adds. "He told us his family used to be in the jewelry business. And he said the Bigfoot Beast's eyes looked like rubies."

"We figured that Skinny had discovered the sapphires in the stream bed," Fred says. "Instead of going to Mr. Walden, he decided to scare people away from the camp. That way he could harvest the sapphires, sell them, and keep the money for himself."

"They really belong to Mr. Walden," Velma explains. "He's going to use the money to keep the campground going. He's even going to help Mindy Podwick study the fossils in peace."

"Mr. Walden's really a happy camper

now, right, Scoob?" Shaggy asks.

Scooby gulps down the last pancake. "*Right!*"

Fred turns to you. "So, how did you do?" Fred asks.

"I bet you did great!" Daphne says. "And don't worry if you didn't. Solving mysteries can be pretty challenging. That's why it takes all of us working together to solve our mysteries."

Scooby-Doo nods his head. "*Roooby-Rooby-Roo!*"

THE CASE OF
THE GLOWING ALIEN

"Hey, come on over!" Fred calls from across the pizza parlor. "It's great to see you."

You close the door to Louie's Pizza Parlor. It's warm inside, and the smell of freshly baked pizza fills the place. You walk over to the big booth in the back where Fred, Velma, Daphne, Shaggy, and Scooby are sitting. Shaggy and Scooby each have a big pile of pizza crusts in front of them.

"Are you ready, Scoob?" Shaggy asks.

"*Ready!*" Scooby says, smiling.

"On the count of three," Shaggy continues. "One. Two. Wait — hold it!" Shaggy looks at you.

"Like, do you wanna join our crust crunching contest?" he asks you.

"Shaggy, we'd like to talk to our friend, if you don't mind," Daphne interrupts.

"Gee, Daph, I was just being friendly," Shaggy replies. "Okay, Scoob, where was I?"

"*Ree!*" Scooby exclaims as he starts devouring the pizza crusts.

"Hey, no fair!" Shaggy yells. Then he starts gobbling up the pizza crusts, too.

"Don't mind them," Velma says. "They've been talking about their crust crunching contest all day."

"All week is more like it," Daphne adds. "Ever since we got back from solving our last mystery."

"And that was some mystery," Fred says. "It was unlike any we've ever had to solve."

You're having a hard time paying attention to Fred, Daphne, and Velma. Shaggy and Scooby are crunching up a storm, and bits of pizza crust are flying everywhere.

"Mmmmumph," Shaggy says with a mouthful of pizza crust.

"What did you say?" Daphne asks.

"Mmm...mummph!" Shaggy says, trying to swallow his mouthful of food.

"You really shouldn't talk with your mouth full," Velma lectures. "It's bad for your digestion."

"I think he's trying to say —" Fred begins.

"*Rinished!*" Scooby says, licking his lips. His plate is clean and his mouth is empty.

"Mumph!" Shaggy says, still working on the food in his mouth.

You smile and congratulate Scooby, giving him a pat on the head.

"Now about that mystery," Fred says. "We sure could've used your help."

"I bet you would've been able to figure it out in no time," Velma says.

Just the thought of solving a mystery brings a smile to your face.

"Judging by your expression," Daphne says, "I think you'd love the chance to solve the mystery, right?"

"You bet!" you say.

"That's great!" Fred says. "Because it just so happens that you can. This is our Clue Keeper for the case."

Fred holds up a small notebook with a patterned cover.

"We call this mystery *The Case of the Glowing Alien*," Fred says as he hands you the notebook.

"We write down everything that happens to us in our Clue Keeper," Daphne explains. "The people we meet, the clues we find, you know, things like that."

"We take turns writing the journal," Fred adds. "I was the writer for this mystery."

"All you have to do is read our Clue Keeper," Velma continues. "We've even added some shortcuts. Whenever you see

this you know you've met a suspect in the case. And whenever you see this
you've found a clue."

"Our Clue Keeper is divided into sec-
tions," Fred says. "At the end of some entries, we'll ask you questions. This will help
you organize the suspects and clues you
find. All you need is your own Clue Keeper
and a pen or pencil."

"So, what do you say?" Daphne asks.
"Are you ready?"

Before you can answer, Shaggy interrupts.

"So, Scooby, how about two out of three?"
he asks.

"*Ro rore room*," Scooby says, shaking his
head and pating his belly.

Shaggy then looks at you. "Like, I'll bet
you're up to a crust crunching contest,
right?" he asks.

"Not now, Shaggy," Fred says. "I think
our friend has something a little more important to do. Right?"

You nod your head in excitement.

"Right!" you exclaim.

Clue Keeper Entry 1

The gang and I arrived at High Point Park for a big picnic celebrating the park's opening. The park sits on top of a large hill, making it the highest point in the county. The park used to be an old dump. Then some people decided to volunteer their time to clean it up.

A lot of people were there that afternoon enjoying the view from the observation platform. Others were playing catch on the great lawn in front of the main pavilion. And still others were there for the food.

"So, like, where's the barbecue?" Shaggy asked.

"Right over there, young man," a woman replied.

It was Cecilia Cornwallis. She's the one who organized all of the volunteers. Cecilia was a tall woman dressed all in green. She wore a yellow scarf tied around her neck.

"The park looks beautiful," Daphne said. "You'd never know what used to be up here."

"Yes, I'm very proud of this park," Cecilia told us. "But I am worried that it may not last very long."

"Why not?" Velma asked.

"Since this was a volunteer effort, we need the town's approval to make it an official park," Cecilia explained. "But there are a lot of people who want the land to be used for other things. I'm afraid that if anything goes wrong today, one of them might just get their way."

"And I'll bet dollars to donuts it'll be me," said a man walking by. He stopped and joined our conversation. "But don't worry, darling. I'll give you full credit. Directed by Sy Stroganoff. Set Design by Cecilia

Cornwallis and her volunteer clean-up brigade." The man laughed.

"Don't laugh, Sy," Cecilia warned. "You may not get your way. And if I have anything to say about it, no one will."

"We'll see, Cecilia," the man said. He turned to us and introduced himself. "I'm Sy Stroganoff. Pleased to meet you."

"Sy Stroganoff?" Shaggy said. "Like, you directed Scooby's and my favorite movie: *Attack of the Crazy Pizza Man*."

"Ah, one of my early classics," Sy said.

"What brings you to High Point Park?" I asked.

"I'm here to direct a movie," Sy said. "This park is the perfect setting. Of course, we'll need to put in some cactus plants. And tear up some of the grass."

"You wouldn't," Cecilia said.

"I probably will," Sy replied. "Especially once the town council realizes how much money and tourism my film will bring to this place."

"Uh, Ms. Cornwallis, you don't look so

well," Daphne said. "Would you like some water or something?"

"A very good idea," Cecilia said. "Please, excuse me." Cecilia walked away.

"Like, what kind of movie are you making, Mr. Stroganoff?" Shaggy asked. *Return of the Crazy Pizza Man?*"

"No," Sy replied. "It's a special movie that requires the unique characteristics of this beautiful park."

"Is it about nature?" Velma asked.

"No, aliens," Sy said. "With lots of special effects. We've even started running wires and things in the trees. They're part of our special effects, you see. Now if you'll excuse me, I must go to the effects trailer and check on the latest version of the alien."

Once Sy Stroganoff walked away, Shaggy said, "Like, I think Scooby and I are ready for a little barbecue. What do you say, pal?"

"*Rou ret!*" agreed Scooby.

Shaggy and Scooby walked over to the food while Daphne, Velma and I went to check out the view.

"**H**ey, did you notice the 👀 back there? That was a tip that you've found your first suspect. Now grab your Clue Keeper and answer the following questions about this suspect."

1. What is the suspect's name?

2. What kind of work does he do?

3. And why is he so interested in the park?

Clue Keeper Entry 2

Shaggy and Scooby walked across the grass toward the barbecues.

"Hey, Scoob, remember that scene from *Attack of the Crazy Pizza Man*?" Shaggy asked. "You know, the one where the Crazy Pizza Man splashes tomato sauce over everybody? They sure don't make movies like that anymore, right, pal? Scooby?"

Shaggy realized that Scooby wasn't paying attention. Scooby was watching a small animal scurry across the grass.

"Scooby, that's just a squirrel," Shaggy said.

"*Ratch ris*," Scooby whispered to Shaggy. Scooby crouched down and crawled very slowly across the grass on his stomach. Just as he was about to stand up and shout "boo!" two men came running over.

"Hey! Stop!" they yelled. The squirrel looked up at Scooby. It made a screeching sound so loud that Scooby had to cover his ears. Then the squirrel jumped up onto Scooby's back. From there, it jumped onto a tree and ran up the trunk, disappearing into the branches. Shaggy ran over to the tree as the two men got there.

"We're sorry we yelled at you," one of them said.

"But we didn't want you to hurt the squirrel," the other added. "They can get upset quite easily."

"Like, are there really two people there?" Shaggy whispered to Scooby. "Or am I seeing double?"

The two men, it turned out, were identical twins.

"We're the Bell Brothers," the other said.

"I'm Don, and this is Ron. We run the local animal shelter."

"So, like, what's the big deal about the squirrel?" Shaggy asked.

"That was no ordinary squirrel," Ron answered. "It was a red-bellied sap squirrel."

"The red-bellied sap squirrel is a very rare breed," Don explained. "It's almost extinct, in fact."

Ron continued, "And this park is the only red-bellied sap squirrel habitat left in this part of the country."

"We've spent a lot of time and money trying to protect these squirrels and their habitat," Don said. "We've put monitoring equipment all over the park so we can keep track of them. Look up in that tree there."

Don pointed to a small black box hidden among the branches of the tree.

"We're trying to get this park turned into a nature reserve," Don continued. "So the squirrels will have a safe place to live."

"We've even strung wires between the treetops," Ron said. "That way the squirrels can get around without having to walk on the ground. That keeps them safe from their natural enemies."

"Like, who would that be?" Shaggy asked.

"Well, people for one," Ron answered. "They trample in the nuts and berries that the squirrels eat." Then he looked right at Scooby. "But dogs are an even greater threat."

"We submitted a petition to the town council," Don said. "But even if they don't approve it, we'll keep on fighting."

"Don, over there!" Ron said. "Someone's

about to feed a squirrel. Come on!" Ron ran off, followed by Don.

"Speaking of feeding," Shaggy said. "Like, let's go find that barbecue. We still have time for a pre-dinner snack."

Shaggy and Scooby's
Mystery-Solving Tips

"Like, did you see the 👁 👁 in that last entry? Groovy. Now open your Clue Keeper and answer the following questions about this entry."

1. What are the suspects' names?

2. What kind of work do they do?

3. Like, why are they so interested in the park?

"Now go and have a snack!"

Clue Keeper Entry 3

Daphne, Velma, and I stood along the observation platform at one end of the park. The sun was just beginning to set. We looked out over miles and miles of hills and trees.

"Jinkies," Velma exclaimed. "I wonder how far you can see from up here."

"On a clear day you can see for twenty-seven miles," a man said. I looked over and saw a man standing with a telescope.

"Twenty-seven miles straight ahead," the man said. "But thousands of miles straight up." He pointed to the sky.

"Straight up?" Daphne asked. "Hey, are you an astronomer?"

"That's right. My name's Greg Grogan," the man said. "There's no other place like this for miles. You know, I've been begging the town to build an observatory here for years."

"Then you must be happy that this park finally opened," I said.

"Oh, no, no, no," Greg replied. "The last thing I want is a park here. No, what this town needs is a state-of-the-art observatory for mapping other galaxies, and finding comets, and looking for life in space."

"Did you say life in space?" Velma asked.

"Of course," Greg said. "There have been no less than seventeen UFO sightings up here alone. I've seen six of them myself."

I looked at the girls. They looked at me. I could tell they were thinking what I was thinking — this guy was a bit odd to say the least.

"I know what you're thinking," Greg said. "I'm just another loony who's looking for aliens. But mark my words, those aliens will show up and prove I'm right. Before you know it, you'll be looking at the Gregory Grogan Observatory right here. Now if you'll excuse me, I have to find a certain star before the fireworks start."

We had forgotten about the big fireworks show scheduled for that evening. We made our quick good-byes to Greg Grogan and headed back to the center of the park.

"He gave me the creeps," Daphne said.

"Like, did you meet those crazy brothers, too?" Shaggy asked. He and Scooby walked up to the girls and me. They were finishing their barbecue snacks.

"What brothers?" Velma asked. "We were talking about Greg Grogan, that guy looking through the telescope."

"Scooby and I just ran into these two creepy twin brothers," Shaggy said. "Like, they thought Scooby was going to hurt one of their red-bellied sap squirrels."

"That's odd," said Velma.

"Like, I know," Shaggy agreed. "I mean, everybody knows my pal here would never hurt a squirrel. Right, Scoob?"

"Right!" Scooby said.

"No, Shaggy, I mean about the red-bellied sap squirrels," Velma continued. "I've never heard of that kind of squirrel."

"Well, don't tell those brothers," Shaggy said. "They want to turn the park into a nature reserve just to protect them."

"It sounds to me like Cecilia Cornwallis has a lot of reasons to be worried about the park," I said.

"I just hope everything turns out okay," Daphne said.

"Of course it will, Daph," Shaggy said. "Like, what could possibly go wrong?"

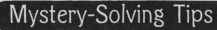

"**D**id you catch the ? Fred and I thought you would. Grab your Clue Keeper and answer the following questions about this suspect."

1. What is the suspect's name?

2. What kind of work does he do?

3. Why is he so interested in the park?

Clue Keeper Entry 4

By this time, it was dark outside. Everyone had gathered on the great lawn in the center of the park for the fireworks show. The gang and I sat down on the grass and waited for the show to begin. One by one, the lights on the lampposts started going out.

"Huh?" Scooby asked.

"Don't worry, Scooby," Daphne said. "They're just turning out the lampposts so we can see the fireworks better, that's all."

"*Rokay,*" Scooby said with relief.

Then a funny sound filled the air.

"Like, I've heard some weird music before," Shaggy said, "but this is the weirdest."

A moment later, a bright light descended from the sky. As it got lower, the strange sound got louder. Suddenly, there was a big flash of light and a huge puff of smoke. The crowd started getting scared.

"I wonder what's going on?" Velma asked.

"Could it be . . . a . . . a . . . spaceship?" Shaggy asked, shaking with fear.

Then, from out of nowhere, a strange looking creature appeared to fly through the air. It had a small round head and long arms with very skinny fingers. And its skin seemed to glow in the dark. The alien started making a strange and scary sound. It was so loud, Scooby had to cover his ears.

"Zoinks! It's a space alien!" Shaggy yelled. "Everybody run!"

The other people sitting on the lawn stood up and ran away screaming. The alien flew back and forth making all kinds of strange sounds. Then it suddenly disappeared.

As people ran out of the park, Cecilia

Cornwallis walked around trying to calm them down. Soon, the gang, Ms. Cornwallis and I were the only ones left.

"I can't believe it," Cecilia said. "Once word spreads about this, they'll close the park for sure. Who would want to come to a park that is haunted by aliens?"

"Wow!" Daphne exclaimed. "Do you think that Greg Grogan could have been right about intelligent life in outer space?"

"I don't know about outer space," I said. "But I do know there's intelligent life right here on Earth. And I think we need to use it to figure out if this alien is for real."

"Fred's right," Daphne said.

"Ms. Cornwallis?" I asked. "Don't worry about a thing. The Mystery, Inc. gang is on the case."

"Thank you, kids," Cecilia said. "Is there anything I can do to help?"

"You can start by turning the lampposts back on," Velma said. "We'll need every bit of light to help us search for clues."

"Would you happen to have any flashlights?" Daphne asked.

"In my car," Cecilia answered. "I'll get them right after I turn the lampposts back on."

"When Cecilia returns with the flashlights, we'll split up to look for clues," Fred said.

Clue Keeper Entry 5

Cecilia Cornwallis returned with four flashlights.

"Thanks, Ms. Cornwallis," Daphne said. "Do you want to join us?"

"No, thank you," Cecilia replied. "I'm still a bit shaken up about the whole thing. I'm going to rest in the main pavilion. Come get me as soon as you find something."

"Daphne and I will check out the other side of the park," I said. "You know, where the spaceship seemed to land."

"Great idea," Velma said. "Shaggy, Scooby and I will look around here for signs of the alien."

"We'll meet back at the main pavilion," I said. "Now let's get started," Fred said. Daphne and I walked off across the great lawn.

"I noticed that the alien only moved between those two tall trees," Velma said. She pointed toward a couple of trees on the opposite side of the lawn.

"Shaggy, Scooby, you two check out that tree," Velma instructed. "I'll look on the other side. If you find anything suspicious, flash your flashlight quickly three times." Velma walked to the other side of the great lawn.

Shaggy shone his flashlight out in front of him and Scooby. They walked quickly to the tree.

"I don't see anything here," Shaggy said. "Do you, Scoob?"

"*Uh-uh,*" Scooby said.

"Oh, well, that's the way it goes," Shaggy said. "At least we tried. What do you say we head back to the pavilion and see if we can get something to eat."

"*Right!*" Scooby said. Shaggy and Scooby

turned and walked toward the main pavilion. On their way, a flashing light caught their attention.

"Like, I think Velma's found something," Shaggy said. They changed direction and walked across the lawn to Velma.

She was standing next to a tree. She shone her flashlight up into the branches.

"Tell me what you see," Velma said.

Shaggy and Scooby looked up.

"Like, a tree, Velma," Shaggy replied.

"No, where my light is shining," Velma said.

"*Reaves*," Scooby answered.

"And branches," Shaggy added.

"Don't you see that small black box up on the branch?" Velma asked. "It's right there."

Shaggy and Scooby looked up again.

"Oh, yeah," Shaggy said. "It looks like a miniature stereo speaker."

"Doesn't that strike you as odd?" Velma asked.

Shaggy thought for a moment.

"Yeah, I guess so," Shaggy said. "Like, why would squirrels be listening to music?" Shaggy said to Scooby.

"My point exactly," Velma said.

"I mean, squirrels don't even have ears," Shaggy continued.

"Oh, brother," Velma said, rolling her eyes at Shaggy's response. "I'm going to see if there are small black boxes in other trees."

"Great," Shaggy said. "Scooby and I will go check out the snack bar — I mean, go meet Fred and Daphne at the main pavilion."

"Just be careful, you two," Velma warned.

"No sweat, Velma," Shaggy said. "Like, we're just walking across the lawn to the main pavilion. What could possibly happen to us between here and there?"

Velma's

Mystery-Solving Tips

"Did you notice the  back there? That's where you'll find your first clue. Open up your Clue Keeper and answer the following questions about it."

1. What clue did you find in this entry?

2. What do you think this clue has to do with the alien?

3. Which of the suspects could have left this clue?

99

Clue Keeper Entry 6

Shaggy and Scooby walked across the grass toward the main pavilion.

"Like, did you hear something, Scoob?" Shaggy asked.

Scooby tilted his head and raised his left ear. Then he slowly moved his head from left to right.

"*Uh-uh*," Scooby reported.

"Must be my imagination," Shaggy said. "For a second, I thought I heard the Crazy Pizza Man following us."

Shaggy and Scooby looked at each other. Then they started walking a little faster.

"Scooby, quit walking so close to me,"

Shaggy complained. "Like, your breath is melting the back of my neck."

"*Rorry,*" Scooby said. Shaggy looked over and saw that Scooby was walking next to him, not behind him.

"Uh, Scoob, since you're not following me," whispered Shaggy. "Can you tell me, like, who is following me?"

Scooby looked at Shaggy and then behind him.

"*Ralien!*" Scooby yelled.

"Zoinks!" Shaggy echoed. "Run, Scoob!"

The alien chased Shaggy and Scooby all the way to the main pavilion. It made terrible screeching sounds. Shaggy and Scooby tried to run inside the main pavilion, but the door was locked. When they turned to run the other way, they noticed the alien was gone.

"Hey, like, he's gone, Scoob," Shaggy said.

Shaggy and Scooby heard someone's footsteps in the grass. They saw some kind of light getting closer.

"Zoinks! It's back!" Shaggy cried. "He's

gonna melt our eyeballs and turn us into rocks! Good-bye, Scoob, old pal." Shaggy closed his eyes tightly. After a minute or two, he opened his right eye to see where the alien was. Daphne and I were standing in front of him.

"Would you mind telling us what you are doing, Shaggy?" Daphne asked.

"Like, the alien chased me and Scooby," Shaggy said.

"Where's Velma?" I asked.

"She was looking for more clues," Shaggy said. "Like, I hope the alien didn't get her."

"We should probably go find her," Daphne said.

"Good idea, Daphne," I said. "Let's go, fellas."

"Oh, no you don't," Shaggy said. "We're not going out there where some alien can chase us and beam its death ray at us."

"Okay," Daphne said. "I just hope that the alien doesn't come back here looking for you two!" She and I walked away.

"*Rait ror rus!*" Scooby called as he and Shaggy ran after us.

As Shaggy and Scooby ran, they sud-

denly tripped on something and went flying into one another. Daphne and I stopped.

"Would you two quit clowning around?" Daphne asked.

"Like, something tripped us," Shaggy said.

"*Reah, ripped rus,*" Scooby agreed.

"Shaggy's right," Velma said. She walked out from behind a tree holding something. "I found this harness attached to a thin cable running between these two trees."

"A harness and cable?" Daphne asked. "What's that doing here?"

"It was used by our alien to appear to fly," Velma explained. "Only when I took the harness down, I accidentally unhooked the cable. That's what Shaggy and Scooby tripped on."

"And now you need to see what Daphne and I found," I said. "Come on."

"Like, Velma found another interesting clue by the  in this entry. Did you find it, too? Great. Now get your Clue Keeper and answer these questions about it. And, like, don't forget to give yourself another snack when you're done."

1. What clue did you find in this entry?

2. What do you think the clue has to do with the alien?

3. Which of the suspects could have put the cables up across the trees?

Clue Keeper Entry 7

The gang and I walked over to the far side of the great lawn. There were two big trees on opposite sides of the grass.

"Now watch closely," I said.

I walked over to one tree, and Daphne to the other.

"Ready, Daph?" I asked.

"Ready," she replied.

I reached up and pulled on a branch. Suddenly, a ball of colorful lights appeared near the top of the tree. The lights then started floating down.

"Zoinks!" Shaggy exclaimed. "It's the alien's spaceship."

"No, it's not, Shaggy," Velma said. "It's just a string of colored lights bunched together."

"I don't care what they are," Shaggy said. "They're flying!"

"Actually, the lights are attached to a very thin wire that extends from the top of that tree to the bottom of this one," Daphne said. "I'm pulling another wire that's making the lights move."

"So, like it's not a spaceship?" Shaggy asked. "That's a relief, right Scoob? Scoob?"

Scooby was holding something. He reached down and touched it with his paw. A loud screeching sound filled the air.

"*Rikes!*" Scooby howled. He jumped up and threw the thing to the ground.

"The alien!" Shaggy yelled.

Velma walked over to where the sound was coming from. She knelt down and picked something up. She pushed a button on it and the sound stopped.

"Scooby, where did you get that?" I asked.

"*Ron ruh rass*," Scooby answered.

Velma looked at it carefully. "That's odd," she said. "This portable cassette player has a built-in loudspeaker."

"Yeah, emphasis on loud," Shaggy said.

"I'll bet the alien dropped it when he was chasing you earlier," Daphne said.

"Things are starting to fall into place," Velma said. "I have a hunch that this alien isn't from another town, much less another planet."

"Velma's right," I said. "It's time to set a trap."

108

"Daphne and I hope you saw the  back there, because this is an important clue. Make sure you answer all of the questions about it in your Clue Keeper."

1. What clue did you find in this entry?

2. What other time do you remember hearing a sound like this?

3. Which suspects were around when you heard that sound?

Clue Keeper Entry 8

The gang and I had a great idea for the trap: we were going to out-alien the alien. First, Velma and Daphne needed to disguise Scooby as an alien. Then Shaggy was supposed to get the alien to chase him across the great lawn. When the alien got to a certain spot, Scooby would fly through the air using the harness and wires that Velma found earlier. Once Scooby startled the alien, Shaggy and I would jump out and capture it in one of the picnic blankets left on the lawn. The only hard part was convincing Scooby-Doo.

"Please, Scooby?" Daphne said. "We'll give you a Scooby Snack."

"*Uh-uh*," Scooby answered. He crossed his paws and looked away.

"Will you do it for two Scooby Snacks?" Velma asked.

"*Mmmmmm*," Scooby thought for a moment. "Rope!"

"All right, three Scooby Snacks," Daphne said. "But that's it."

"*Rokay!*" said Scooby. Daphne and Velma took turns tossing the three Scooby Snacks into the air. Scooby jumped up and gobbled down each one.

We were finally able to spring into action. Daphne and Velma took Scooby aside and started putting together an alien disguise. I walked with Shaggy toward the main pavilion.

"Remember, Shaggy, just make sure you run to the right trees," I said.

"Like, I'm so scared that any tree where there isn't an alien is the right tree for me," Shaggy replied.

"Then don't think about the alien," I coaxed. "Pretend you're being chased by the Crazy Pizza Man instead."

"The Crazy Pizza Man?" Shaggy said. "No one's afraid of the Crazy Pizza Man. He's, like, made out of pizza crusts and burnt cheese."

"That's great, Shaggy," I said. "If you get scared, think of the Crazy Pizza Man." I turned and left Shaggy alone. Inside, I was holding my breath hoping that he wouldn't mess up the plans.

"Oh, I'm not scared," Shaggy called. "But thanks to all that talk about the Crazy Pizza Man, now I'm hungry."

Shaggy stood on the grass and looked around. It was pretty quiet.

"Hey, alien, come out, come out, from wherever you are," Shaggy called. "Like, maybe he flew back to his planet." Shaggy walked across the lawn. After a few steps,

Shaggy felt that same hot breath on the back of his neck.

"Gulp," Shaggy swallowed hard. He turned his head just a bit and caught a glimpse of a greenish face and long slender fingers.

"Zoinks!" Shaggy exlaimed. "Coming through!" Shaggy started running. The alien chased him all over the great lawn.

"Pssssst, Shaggy!" Daphne whispered from the trees. "This way!" She pointed toward the middle of the great lawn.

Shaggy started running in that direction.

Suddenly, a strange-looking creature flew out of nowhere and across the sky.

"Zoinks!" Shaggy yelled. "It's another one!" He turned and started running in the opposite direction. I quickly caught Shaggy's attention and waved him over behind a tree.

The alien who was chasing Shaggy saw the flying alien, who was really Scooby in disguise. Scooby then made some strange alien sounds.

114

"*Rooooooooooo,*" Scooby moaned.

The alien stared at Scooby. It reached its hand up and tried to grab Scooby's foot.

"*Rikes!*" Scooby yelled.

Very quietly, Shaggy and I held a picnic blanket and snuck up behind the alien. Just as we were about to throw the blanket over the alien, we heard something snap. Shaggy had stepped on a branch.

The alien whipped around and let out a big screech, startling us. Suddenly, everyone heard the flying alien say, *"Roooooby-Rooby-Roo!"*

The alien looked up and saw Scooby unfasten his harness. Before the glowing alien could run away, Scooby landed right on top of him with a thud.

Cecilia Cornwallis ran across the lawn with Daphne and Velma.

"You've caught him!" Cecilia exclaimed. "How wonderful."

"Would you like to see who's behind all this?" Daphne asked.

"Absolutely, dear," Cecilia replied. She reached over and pulled the alien's mask right off his head.

"**H**ey, who ordered the spaghetti pizza?" Louie shouts from behind the counter.

You look up from reading the gang's Clue Keeper.

"Well, now you've met all the suspects and found all the clues," Fred says. "Do you think you're up to solving the mystery?"

You nod your head.

"Great," Daphne says. "Here's some advice. Look at your list of suspects and clues and answer these questions."

"First, who do you think had a good reason to scare people away from the park?" Velma asks.

"Second, who do you think had the know-how to scare people away from the park?" Fred asks.

"Third, who do you think had the opportunity to scare people away from the park?" Daphne asks.

"See if you can eliminate any of the suspects first," Velma suggests. "Then using all of the information you've collected, as well as your own smarts, try to figure out who the alien really is."

"Like, anybody want some?" Shaggy asks as Louie puts a huge plate in front of him and Scooby. "Louie makes the best spaghetti pizza around."

"Why don't you solve the mystery while Shaggy and Scooby are having their snack?" Daphne suggests. "Then when you're done, we'll tell you who was behind all the antics."

"Jinkies! It's your last chance to solve the mystery before the gang reveals the answer. When you're ready, turn the page to read the groovy ending of The Case of the Glowing Alien."

"The Bell Brothers were behind the whole thing," Velma says. "Don wore the alien costume, and Ron operated the fake spaceship and the lights and the pulleys to make Don fly."

"You know that our other two suspects were Greg Grogan, the amateur astronomer," Daphne says.

"And Sy Stroganoff," Fred adds. "All of the suspects had reasons for wanting to keep people away from the park."

"After thinking about it a bit, we decided Greg Grogan couldn't have had anything to do with the mystery," Daphne says. "After all, he's the only suspect who truly believed in intelligent life on other planets. He wouldn't want people to think that aliens were mean and scary."

"That left the Bell Brothers and Sy Stroganoff," Fred says. "They all had access to the park to put up wires and speakers and things."

"After all, Sy Stroganoff said he was already preparing for his movie shoot," Daphne says. "And the Bell Brothers said they put up monitors and cables for the squirrels."

"Mr. Stroganoff could have used his movie equipment to make the alien and all the effects," Fred explains. "Or the Bell Brothers could have used their monitors as loudspeakers and stolen the rest from Mr. Stroganoff's storage truck."

"The clue that tipped us off was the portable tape player that Scooby found," Velma says. "It was supposed to be the alien's voice. But the sound on that tape is definitely not from outer space. Right, Scooby?"

"*Right!*" agrees Scooby.

"The Bell Brothers had recorded the squirrel sounds and used them to make the alien's screeches," Daphne explains. "All in the name of preserving the red-bellied sap squirrel."

Just then, a red-bellied sap squirrel jumps up from under the table and sits next to the spaghetti pizza and Scooby. The squirrel takes a nibble of the pizza crust and screeches happily.

"And turning their nature reserve into an all-squirrel zoo that they hoped to make money on," Fred adds.

Everyone across the table now looks at you.

"So, how did you do?" Daphne asks.

"I'll bet you solved the mystery without any problem," Velma adds with a smile. "After all, you do have some pretty good teachers."

"Like, solving mysteries isn't all you can learn from us," Shaggy says to you.

"Really?" Daphne asks. "What else is there?"

"Like, the best way to eat a spaghetti pizza," Shaggy says.

He and Scooby each take a huge bite of the spaghetti pizza. As they slurp up the spaghetti, you notice that they are eating opposite ends of the same piece. Shaggy and Scooby both try to slurp the spaghetti into their mouths. Suddenly, the red-bellied sap squirrel jumps up and takes a bite out of the middle. The ends of the spaghetti quickly disappear into Shaggy's and Scooby's mouths. The squirrel chews happily.

"Come back and visit us again," Fred says. "There's always another mystery to solve."

"And, like, another pizza to eat," Shaggy says. "Right, Scoob?"

"*Rooooooby-Rooby-Roo!*" Scooby agrees.

THE CASE OF
THE SEAWEED MONSTER

You glance at your watch and see that you're late. You start running down the street, trying not to bump into anybody. You turn the corner and have to stop short.

A long line of people stretches down the street in front of you. You start walking down the street and then hear someone call your name. You look up and see Daphne waving at you from the front of the line.

"Hurry, we're next!" she shouts. You run the rest of the way down the street and meet up with Daphne, Fred, Velma, Shaggy, and Scooby-Doo.

"Next!" yells a voice from inside the door.

"Like, that's us!" Shaggy exclaims. "Let's go, Scooby-Doo!"

Scooby jumps up and runs inside with Shaggy before the rest of you take one step.

You follow Fred, Daphne, and Velma inside the restaurant and look around. It's not very big. There's a row of about ten round tables along the left side of the restaurant. Along the right side is a serving line. A waiter leads you and the gang to a table in the back.

"This place has the best soup," Daphne says. "And there are no menus. They just keep bringing you different soups until you tell them to stop."

"Like, that's great, Daph," Shaggy says. "But what else do they have?"

"That's it, Shaggy," Daphne says. "Just soup."

"You mean people actually wait in line just to have soup?" Shaggy asks.

"Shaggy, people will wait in line for any-

130

thing that's special," Velma says. "Like at the aquarium the other day."

"Man, don't bring that up," Shaggy moans. The waiter puts a bowl of soup in front of Scooby.

"Rikes!" he yells and dives under the table.

"What's the matter?" Daphne asks.

Scooby's tail pops up. He changes it into an arrow and points at his bowl of soup.

"There's nothing in there but some Chinese cabbage," Velma says.

"That's not cabbage," Shaggy says. "That's seaweed! Make way, Scoob!" He dives under the table, too.

Fred, Daphne, and Velma all smile and shake their heads.

"They're just being silly," Daphne says. "Something in the soup reminds them of our last mystery."

"It was a real interesting one," Fred continues. "I'll bet you would have loved to helped us solve it."

"You still can, you know," Velma suggests. "Why don't you read our Clue Keeper and see if you can figure out the mystery, too?" She reaches into her pocket and takes out a small notebook. "Everything you need to know is in there," she says. "I should know because I took the notes this time."

"Remember, when you see 👁👁 you've just met a suspect," Daphne says.

"And a 🔦 tells you that you've just found a clue," continues Fred. "After each entry, we'll ask you some questions to help you along."

"So keep your own Clue Keeper and a pencil handy," Velma says. "And good luck solving *The Case of the Seaweed Monster.*"

132

Clue Keeper Entry 1

We had just arrived at the Harbor View Aquarium to see the new dolphin show. We had to wait in the van for a few minutes for the rain to stop.

"Man, I can't believe Scoob and I had to miss the pizza eating contest at Luigi's just to go see some stupid dolphins," Shaggy complained.

133

"Actually, Shaggy, dolphins are believed to be the smartest mammals on the planet," I said.

"*Ruh-uh,*" Scooby disagreed.

"Scooby's right," Shaggy said. "Everyone knows that *people* are the smartest mammals. Right, Scoob?"

Scooby shook his head back and forth.

"Then who's smarter than dolphins and people?" I asked.

"*Rogs!*" shouted Scooby gleefully.

"Oh, brother!" Daphne exclaimed with a smile. "I can't wait to see this new dolphin show. They say the show features the statue of a golden dolphin that's just been brought up from the ocean floor."

"Like, I read about that in the newspaper," Shaggy said. "Isn't that statue supposed to have some kind of an ancient South Sea Island curse on it?"

"I read that, too," Daphne told Shaggy. "That just makes it even more interesting."

"Okay, everyone, it looks like the rain is letting up," Fred said. "Let's go in while we have the chance."

We got out of the van and ran across the parking lot to the aquarium entrance. There was a long line of people standing under the canopy just outside the building. Many of them were dressed in green ponchos. I knew the ponchos had been purchased at the aquarium gift store, because I had one myself that I'd bought the last time I was there. I sure wished I had it with me.

As we got closer, we noticed a man in a green poncho. He smiled and chatted with all the damp people in line. When he saw us approach, he turned and smiled at us.

"Good afternoon," he said cheerily. "Welcome to the Harbor View Aquarium. I'm Jonah Bellows, the aquarium's director. I've just been telling folks about our great new dolphin show. You must see it."

"I don't know," Shaggy said. "Is that gold statue in the dolphin tank really cursed?"

Mr. Bellows scowled. "You read that in the newspaper, didn't you?" he said. "That article is killing my business. I think it's all part of a plot to shut down this aquarium!"

"Why would you think that?" Daphne asked. "Have other things been happening?"

Mr. Bellows looked around to see if anyone was listening. "Yes," he replied. "Very strange things."

"Zoinks!" cried Shaggy. "It's the Curse of the Golden Dolphin!"

"Shhhh!" Mr. Bellows shushed him. "Please don't say that so loud! It will frighten the other visitors."

The gang and I exchanged glances. I'm sure we were all thinking the same thing. Here was another mystery for us to solve.

A woman came up behind us in line. "Don't go in there!" she said so loudly that it was almost a shout. "Whatever you do. Don't enter that aquarium!"

We all turned around and faced her. She

had long, straight black hair and dark eyes.

"Not you again! Would you please keep your voice down?" Mr. Bellows said to her.

"I will not keep my voice down," the woman replied. "People have a right to know the truth!"

"The truth about what?" I asked.

"The truth about the way Jonah Bellows and his staff take advantage of dolphins for personal gain," the woman said.

"I don't understand," Daphne said.

"Allow me to explain," Mr. Bellows interjected before the woman could reply. "This is Carol Reef, from the Sea Creatures Defense Fund. She believes that we mistreat the dolphins that live in the aquarium."

"That's right," Carol said. "They train the dolphins to help find things out at sea. Things like sunken treasures and other valuables. Then Jonah and his people get rich while all the dolphins get is a bucket of fish."

"I'm sure these young people would rather go inside than listen to us," Mr. Bellows said. He reached beneath his poncho and into his

coat pocket. His hand came out holding some small cards.

"Here, take these," he said, handing us the cards. "These are VIP passes. Show them to the security guards and they'll take care of you. Enjoy your visit."

"Thanks, Mr. Bellows," Fred said, taking the cards. "Let's go, gang."

We continued on our way to the front doors. Jonah Bellows and Carol Reef started arguing again. We heard Carol say one last thing to Mr. Bellows.

"I don't care what you say, you're going to stop what you're doing!" she shouted. "Even if it means I have to find some way to close this aquarium down all by myself!"

"Jinkies, she sure was angry, wasn't she? There's no way you could have missed the 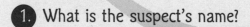 in this entry. So open up your Clue Keeper, grab a pen or pencil, and start your entry for the first suspect by answering these questions."

1. What is the suspect's name?

2. What is she doing at the aquarium?

3. Why do you think she is so angry at Jonah Bellows?

"Once you're done taking your own notes, read on!"

139

Clue Keeper Entry 2

We walked into the aquarium and showed the passes to the security guard. He nodded his head and pointed to a silver door next to the information booth.

"Right through there, folks," he said. "If anyone asks, show them the passes. Just stay away from the restricted areas."

"Like, how will we know which are the re-stricted areas?" Shaggy asked.

"You'll see big signs that say, 'restricted area,'" the guard replied with a smile. "Enjoy your visit."

"Thanks," I said. "Let's go, gang."

We opened the silver door and walked into a brightly lit corridor. There was a long staircase leading down to another door. We walked through that door.

"Jinkies!" I exclaimed as I looked around. "This is amazing!"

The wall in front of us looked like it was made of glass. We could see right through it into a huge tank of water.

"Man, that's the largest indoor swimming pool I've ever seen!" Shaggy added.

"Shaggy, that's not a swimming pool," Daphne said. "That's the dolphin tank be-hind that glass!"

We all looked up and saw three dolphins swimming right toward us.

"Actually, it's a special kind of see-through plastic called plexiglass," we heard

Jonah Bellows say. He walked over to us. "It's several inches thick, so you don't have to worry about any dolphins — or water — getting out."

Scooby crept up to the tank. He got closer and closer until his nose and front paws were pressed against the plexiglass. A dolphin suddenly swam up and pressed his nose against the inside of the tank.

"*Rikes!*" Scooby yelled as he jumped back.

"Relax, Scooby," I said. "He's only play-

ing. More proof that dolphins really are smarter than dogs."

"What happened to Carol Reef?" Daphne asked.

"I got tired of being yelled at so I came back inside," Mr. Bellows replied. "I'm sure I haven't heard the last of her."

"Mr. Bellows, is that someone in the tank with the dolphins?" I asked.

We all got closer to get a better look. We could see a figure in the water.

"That's Gil Gupperman," Jonah said. "He's my assistant. Right now, he's putting the finishing touches on our newest display."

We watched as the figure made a sudden gesture with his arms. He spun around as one of the dolphins swam past him. The figure waved his arms and tried to grab one of the dolphins. Then he gave up and swam over to one side of the tank. A moment later, we heard a hissing sound.

"That's the air lock," Mr. Bellows explained. "There's a small chamber that connects the tank with this room. When

Gil goes in, he closes the door. The water is pumped out and air is pumped in. When the outer door opens, it makes the hissing sound."

Gil Gupperman stepped out of the air lock.

"That's it, I've had it!" he yelled at Mr. Bellows. "Those dolphins are out to get me!"

"They're not out to get you, Gil," Mr. Bellows said calmly. "They're just playing."

"I don't care what they're doing," Gil complained. "They treat me as badly as you do. I've been working here eight years. It's bad enough I'm still cleaning fish tanks and doing underwater maintenance. Now I have to be teased by dolphins. I don't care how much treasure those overgrown guppies found, I'm not going to take it anymore!"

"Uh, Gil, let's not get excited now," Mr. Bellows tried to calm him. "Why don't you and I have a little talk in private?"

"No more talks!" Gil ordered. "I want things to change around here or there'll be trouble. And lots of it!" Gil took a white card out of his pocket. He slid it through a black box beside a door with a "restricted" sign on it. We heard a clicking sound. Gil opened the door, went inside, and slammed the door shut behind him.

"When he mentioned treasure, was he referring to the golden dolphin?" Fred asked.

"Well, kids, I guess I have some explaining to do," Jonah said with a sigh.

"That was quite a moment, wasn't it? Did you catch the 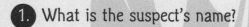 ? Great. Open up your Clue Keeper and answer these questions."

1. What is the suspect's name?

2. What does he do at the aquarium?

3. Why do you think he's so angry at Jonah Bellows?

"Once you've jotted down your notes, read on to find out what Jonah Bellows had to say."

Clue Keeper Entry 3

Jonah Bellows pointed to the dolphin tank.

"If you look closely, you can see something in the middle of the tank," he said.

We all got close to the plexiglass and looked inside.

"I think I see something," Daphne said.

"No, that's just a dolphin," I said.

"You're both right," Mr. Bellows remarked. "It's a dolphin, but it's made out of solid gold."

"The Golden Dolphin?" Shaggy asked. "As in fourteen carats?"

"Eighteen, actually," a voice said from behind us.

We all turned around and saw a tall man wearing a white lab coat. He had very thick, round eyeglasses.

"Ah, Dr. Piedmont," Mr. Bellows said. "Dr. Piedmont is our visiting dolphin expert."

Dr. Piedmont frowned when he heard this.

"Please, Jonah, I am more than a dolphin expert," he said. "You are

148

forgetting that I am the one who found the Golden Dolphin."

"No, the dolphins found the Golden Dolphin," Mr. Bellows corrected.

"Because I trained the dolphins to hunt for treasure," Dr. Piedmont continued. "And I also had the map of where to look."

"Yes, but the aquarium funded the expedition," Mr. Bellows countered. "You are just a short-term, temporary employee of the aquarium. You've only been here a matter of months."

"The most important few months in the history of this aquarium!" Dr. Piedmont shouted.

We could tell that Jonah Bellows and Dr. Piedmont were about to get into an ugly fight.

"Excuse me, Dr. Piedmont," I interrupted. "Is it true that dolphins are the smartest mammals?"

"Of course, young lady," Dr. Piedmont replied. "That is why I work with them. And that is why they were able to find the treasure. And that is why I deserve a bigger reward for my efforts."

"So, that is what this is about?" Mr. Bellows asked. "You want to share in the profits from the Golden Dolphin? Let me tell you something, Dr. Piedmont. The Golden Dolphin will not be sold. It will remain a permanent part of the aquarium's exhibit. And if you don't like it, I suggest you think about finding work some place else!"

Jonah Bellows abruptly left.

"He doesn't know with whom he is dealing," Dr. Piedmont grumbled.

"Excuse me for asking," Daphne said quietly. "But what's so special about the Golden Dolphin?"

"Aside from the fact that it's made of gold?" Fred added.

"Legend has it that it is over three hundred years old," Dr. Piedmont explained. "A tribe of South Sea natives thought it brought them luck. But then a band of pirates stole it from the natives. At first, the pirates planned to sell it, but, later they actually tossed it off their pirate ship when they discovered the curse."

Shaggy and Scooby suddenly turned around.

"Like, d-d-did you say c-c-curse?" Shaggy asked nervously. "You mean . . . it's true?"

"Yes, the curse is very real," Dr. Piedmont continued. "The natives put a curse on the statue so that whoever has it will be haunted by a mysterious sea creature. But I don't believe in curses. I only believe in being fairly rewarded for one's work. Mark my words, I'll see to it that Jonah Bellows gives me my due, or else! Now if you'll excuse me, I have some work to do."

Dr. Piedmont walked away from us. He took a card from his pocket and swiped it through the electronic lock.

"Ladies and gentlemen," came a voice from a loudspeaker. "The dolphin show will start in five minutes."

"Well, gang," Fred said. "Let's get out of here and go watch the show."

"And maybe we can stop at the snack bar along the way," Shaggy said. "Swimming always makes me hungry."

152

"But you haven't been swimming," Daphne said.

"I know, but those dolphins have," Shaggy replied. "Just watching them is enough to work up an appetite!"

"I'll bet you saw the  in this entry, right? Great. So look over these questions and write down the answers in your Clue Keeper."

1. What is the suspect's name?

2. What is his connection to the aquarium?

3. Why is he so angry at Jonah Bellows?

"Once you're done, read on to find out what happened next."

154

Clue Keeper Entry 4

We left the tank area the way we came in. Once we were back in the aquarium lobby, we followed the signs to the dolphin show. We walked through an archway and into an outdoor theater. We showed our passes to one of the aquarium employees. He led us to special seats right up front and handed us five small green packages.

"*Runch!*" Scooby shouted happily. He ripped open the package and unfolded a big green poncho.

"Ruh?" Scooby said.

"That's a poncho, Scooby," I said. "You're supposed to put it on just in case we get splashed during the show."

We all put on our ponchos and looked around.

"Wow!" Daphne exclaimed. "The dolphin tank looks even bigger from up here."

And it was. Downstairs, we only saw part of the bottom of the tank. But when we were sitting in the theater, we saw the whole top of the tank. It must have been as big as a football field. And there was a big dock on the other side of the tank where the dolphin trainers stood.

"Ladies and gentlemen, welcome to Dolphin World at the Harbor View Aquarium!" boomed a voice from the loudspeaker. "Please welcome the royal dolphin family!" The three dolphins in the tank jumped out of the water and tumbled through the air be-

fore splashing back down. Some of the water splashed us.

"Now aren't you glad you didn't eat your poncho?" Daphne asked Scooby with a smile.

The show continued for several minutes. The voice over the loudspeaker introduced the various tricks. The trainers made gestures with their arms and hands. Then the dolphins jumped through hoops, played basketball, or did other kinds of flips, leaps, and fancy tricks.

"And now, please welcome the latest addition to the royal family," the voice announced. "It was freed from its resting place on the bottom of the ocean by its real-life cousins. Ladies and gentlemen, please welcome the Golden Dolphin."

A huge fountain of water sprayed up in the center of the dolphin tank. The three dolphins swam around and around in a big circle. Slowly, something started rising out of the water. It was hard to see with all the splashing and spraying, but it looked like the Golden Dolphin.

"Hey, there's something on the Golden Dolphin," Fred said.

"It looks like a really big clump of sea-weed to me," I said.

"Man, like they couldn't even clean off the statue before they showed it to everyone?" Shaggy asked.

Then the seaweed started to move.

Everyone in the audience gasped.

The seaweed slowly stood up until it was standing on top of the Golden Dolphin. Now it looked more like some kind of creature than just a pile of seaweed.

The creature slowly looked around and then let out a mighty roar.

"Aaaaaaahhhhhhhhrrrrrrrrr!" it bellowed, its voice filling the amphitheater. "Free the Golden Dolphin, or else!!!" it shouted in a creaky, scary voice.

"Zoinks!" Shaggy exclaimed. "Like, the seaweed's talking! The curse has come true. Let's get out of here, Scooby!"

"Right!" Scooby agreed. He and Shaggy stood up to run away, but it was too late. Everyone else in the amphitheater also had that idea. As the people rushed out yelling, Jonah Bellows ran out onto the dock.

"Wait! Wait!" he shouted. "It's all part of the show! Come back, please!" But it was too

late. Everyone was gone. And when we looked back at the Golden Dolphin, so was the seaweed monster.

Fred, Daphne, and I looked at each other and shook our heads. Mr. Bellows was lying. His panicked expression told us that much. This wasn't part of the show at all.

"Hey, Mr. Bellows!" Fred called. "Don't worry about a thing. Mystery, Inc. is on the case!"

Clue Keeper Entry 5

The first thing we wanted to do was get a closer look at the Golden Dolphin itself. We left our seats and followed the walkway around to the other side of the dolphin tank. Jonah Bellows was still standing there, looking around.

"I can't believe it," he sighed. "It was bad

enough that people heard about the curse on the Golden Dolphin. Once word gets out about this seaweed monster, I'll be ruined. No one's going to visit an aquarium with a cursed statue and a monster."

"And, like, that includes us," Shaggy said. "Let's go, Scooby-Doo. We're outta here."

"Oh, no you don't," I said to them. "We're going to need your help finding clues. It's the least we can do to repay Mr. Bellows for the free passes he gave us."

"If it's all right with you, Mr. Bellows," Fred said. "We'd like to look around."

"Sure, why not?" Mr. Bellows said. "I can use all the help I can get."

"Great!" Fred said. "Daphne and I will look around up here to see if there's any sign of the monster."

"Shaggy, Scooby, and I will go back downstairs," I said. "If that seaweed monster came up with the statue, we'll be able to see any clues in the tank through the plexiglass."

"Good idea, Velma," Daphne said. "Let's all meet back here as soon as we can."

"Let's go, boys," I said to Shaggy and Scooby.

"Like, do you think we can stop at the snack bar on the way down," Shaggy said as we left the amphitheater. "We never did quite make it there before the dolphin show."

"We'll see about that later," I said. "Right now we have more important things to do."

"More important than eating?!" Shaggy exclaimed. "Like, in my book, there's no such thing."

"That's because your book is a cookbook," I replied. We walked down the short flight of stairs and opened the metal door.

"I'm going to see if there's anything suspicious in the tank," I continued. "You two see if anything catches your eye out here."

I walked over to the tank and peered through the thick plexiglass. I could see the dolphins swimming around. I could also see the elevated platform holding the Golden Dolphin. But there was no sign of anything else.

"Did you two find anything yet?" I asked

Shaggy and Scooby as I turned around. But instead of looking for clues, Shaggy and Scooby were gone.

"I'll bet they went to the snack bar after all." I sighed. Then I heard a sound coming from the end of the hall. It was some kind of thumping. As I walked down the hall, the thumping grew louder. Then I heard some muffled voices.

I reached the end of the hall and stood in front of a door. The thumping and voices were coming from behind it.

"Oh, no," I groaned. "Shaggy and Scooby are in the air lock."

There were no handles on the door, so I couldn't just open it. I noticed one of the security card locks mounted on the wall next to the door. Without a card, I couldn't open the door.

But I'll bet there's some kind of emergency release, I thought to myself. I looked a little more closely and found a hidden red emergency button. I pushed it and heard a hiss and a click, and then the door opened. Shaggy and Scooby came tumbling out.

"Boy, are we glad to see you, Velma," Shaggy gasped.

"What happened?" I asked.

"Scooby and I were looking for clues. We thought we saw something in there. So we stepped inside, and then the door closed behind us. Man, that was really freaky."

Just then, something green on the floor caught my eye. I picked it up and looked at it carefully.

"Like, that's what we saw," Shaggy said.

"Rat ris rit?" asked Scooby.

166

"I'm not sure, Scooby," I answered. "It looks like seaweed, but it feels like plastic.  I wonder if it's a piece of something. If you ask me, I think we've found our first clue. Let's go tell Fred and Daphne."

"Like, did you catch the  in that last entry? Yeah, it wasn't too hard to miss. So grab your Clue Keeper and answer these questions about it."

1. What is the clue you just found?

2. What do you think this clue has to do with the sea-weed monster?

3. Who else do you remember wearing something that looks and feels like that?

168

Clue Keeper Entry 6

Fred, Daphne, and Mr. Bellows were standing on the dock at the far end of the big, outdoor dolphin tank. They were looking at something in Fred's hand. Daphne looked up, saw us, and waved at us to hurry up. When we got there, Fred showed us what he was holding.

"So, like, you found a credit card," Shaggy said. "What's the big deal?"

"This is not a credit card, Shaggy," Daphne said. "It's a security card. And the big deal is what this security card unlocks."

"Daphne's right," Fred added. "We found it on the ground next to the tank. The seaweed monster must've lost it by accident."

"But we didn't see the seaweed monster come out of the tank," I said. "How could it drop anything out here?"

"We think he dropped it while he was in the tank," Daphne explained. "And it got sprayed out by the fountain of water when the Golden Dolphin came up."

"Of course!" I exclaimed. "That makes perfect sense."

"Man, Scoob and I can't take the suspense anymore," Shaggy blurted out. "What does the card unlock?"

"The lab room downstairs," Mr. Bellows replied. "And the air lock."

"Hmm, interesting," I said. "Now take a look at this."

I showed Fred, Daphne, and Mr. Bellows

the piece of green plastic material Shaggy found in the air lock.

"Why, this looks like it came from one of the aquarium ponchos," Mr. Bellows said.

"Now imagine a whole costume made up of these little pieces of green poncho," I said. "Now what do you get?"

"Zoinks! The seaweed monster!" Shaggy exclaimed.

"Very good, Shaggy," I said. "How did you guess?"

"I didn't!" Shaggy replied in a shaky voice. "It's the seaweed monster! For real!"

We all whirled around and saw the seaweed monster running right toward us!

"Quick, everyone, let's get out of here!" Fred called.

"Follow me!" Mr. Bellows called as he ran toward the seats on the other side of the dolphin tank. We followed him down a narrow passageway under the seats. There were a lot of stairs. We went through a door, and the next thing we knew, we were back downstairs by the dolphin tank.

"Man, does every staircase in this place lead back here?" Shaggy asked.

"Only the ones around the amphitheater," Mr. Bellows replied. "But they're all pretty much hidden and off limits to regular visitors."

"If there's more than one staircase," Daphne said, "that means the seaweed monster must have used one of the others to scare us."

"Things are starting to make sense now," I said. "I have a hunch that our seaweed monster is about to be all washed up."

"Velma's right," Fred agreed. "Gang, it's time to set a trap."

173

Daphne's Mystery-Solving Tips

"**W**ow, so much happened in this entry! Did you find both ? Great! Now open up your Clue Keeper and answer these questions about the clues you found."

1. What clues did you find?

2. What do they have to do with the seaweed monster?

3. Which of the suspects would most likely have access to the clues on a regular basis?

"I know it's a lot of stuff to think about, but I know you can handle it! Now read the next entry to see how we caught the seaweed monster."

Clue Keeper Entry 7

We decided that the best way to lure the seaweed monster back was to continue with the dolphin show. Once the Golden Dolphin made its appearance, the monster was sure to come back and try to scare us again. Mr. Bellows said he'd help us and went to get the dolphins ready.

"Like, sounds like a good plan," Shaggy said. "But what's the catch?"

"There's no catch," Daphne said.

"Oh, yes there is," Shaggy said shaking his head. "There's always a catch. And it usually involves me and Scooby."

"Well, Shaggy . . ." Fred began.

"Here we go," Shaggy moaned.

"I'll need your help on the far side of the tank," Fred said. "That way, when the seaweed monster runs by, we can use the big nets over there to catch him."

"Rand ree?" Scooby asked.

"Scooby, you have the easiest job," I said. "All you have to do is take a short run."

"Ruh?" Scooby asked, sitting up.

"That's not such a big deal for a brave dog like you, right Scooby?" Daphne said to him.

"Ruh-uh," Scooby disagreed. He crossed his paws.

"I know what will make him even braver," I said. "How about a Scooby Snack?"

Scooby licked his lips.

"Rokay!" he agreed.

I tossed a Scooby Snack into the air and he gobbled it down.

Mr. Bellows came back over to the rest of us.

"Everything's ready," he said. "I'll be over here to handle the dolphins."

"Great," Fred said. "Shaggy and I will hide at the other end with those big nets. Scooby, you wait with Mr. Bellows. When the seaweed monster appears, get him to chase you down to us."

"Right!" Scooby replied, saluting Fred like a soldier.

"Daphne and I will sit in the VIP box and cheer," I said. "That way, the seaweed monster will think there's a real show going on."

We all took our places. The voice over the loudspeaker came back on to narrate the show. Mr. Bellows raised his arms above his head and the dolphins suddenly jumped out of the water. They each turned a double flip and splashed back into the tank. Soon, the water started bubbling and fountains of water sprayed up into the air. The Golden Dolphin slowly rose to the surface. Daphne and I cheered and applauded.

Suddenly, we heard a noise come from under our seats. The seaweed monster ran out from one of the secret passages beneath the stands. It raised its seaweedy arms and let out a terrible howl.

"Rikes!" Scooby shouted. Scooby started to run and the seaweed monster started to chase him.

As Scooby ran, his paws slipped on the puddles left over from the big dolphin splashes. He slid along the ground right past where Fred and Shaggy were hiding. The seaweed monster also lost his footing.

Fred and Shaggy threw the net down but the seaweed monster was sliding too fast.

"Ruh-oh!" Scooby gasped. He and the seaweed monster slid off the dock and onto a short diving board extending over the dolphin tank.

SPLASH!

Scooby started dog paddling as hard as he could. The seaweed monster swam after him. Just as the seaweed monster was about to grab Scooby's tail, the monster suddenly shot into the air.

It splashed back into the tank and then went up again. Two of the dolphins were tossing the monster around like a beach ball! The other dolphin swam under Scooby and took him back to the side of the tank. Fred and Shaggy helped him out.

"Ranks!" Scooby thanked the dolphin.

As Daphne and I ran over, we saw one of the dolphins flip the seaweed monster high into the air. The monster sailed through the air and landed right in the dolphin netting at the far end of the tank.

"Man, talk about a perfect catch," Shaggy said.

We all ran over to the netting.

"Now let's see who's really behind all this," Fred said.

"That was some adventure, wasn't it?" says Daphne. "And now that you've finished reading the Clue Keeper, I'll bet you're ready to solve the mystery."

"Open up your own Clue Keeper and take a look at your notes," Fred suggests. "Review your list of suspects to refresh your memory."

"Then look at your clues," Velma continues. "Try to figure out which of the suspects go with each of the clues. I'm sure things will come together pretty quickly."

"Once you've figured it out for yourself, we'll give you the real solution to the mystery," Daphne says.

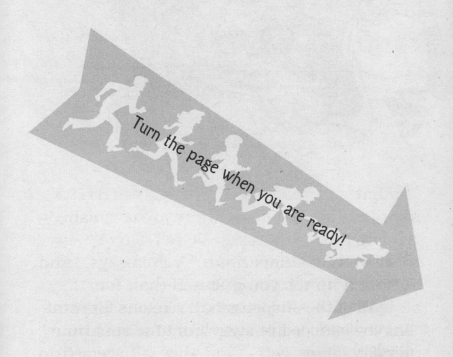

Turn the page when you are ready!

"It was Gil Gupperman," Velma says. "And I have a hunch you guessed that, too."

"All of the suspects had reasons for wanting to scare people away from the aquarium," Fred reminds you. "And they all seemed to want to get revenge on Jonah Bellows. That's why the clues were so important."

"Remember the first clue?" Daphne asks.

184

"That piece of green plastic was cut from one of the green aquarium ponchos. In fact, the seaweed monster's whole costume was made from a bunch of ponchos."

"But any one of the suspects could have done that," Fred says. "Even Carol Reef could have bought the ponchos at the gift shop."

"And since both Dr. Piedmont and Gil Gupperman worked at the aquarium," Velma adds, "they would be able to get their hands on them at any time."

"The second clue we found was the security pass card," Daphne says. "And only an aquarium employee would have one of those. That eliminated Carol Reef."

"But still kept suspicion on Dr. Piedmont and Gil," Fred says. "It wasn't until the last clue that everything fell into place."

"The last clue was knowing about the secret staircases down to the underground rooms. And only a full-time aquarium employee would know about those," Daphne says.

"Dr. Piedmont was only a visitor to the aquarium, remember?" Fred asks. "That left only Gil Gupperman."

"It looks like you solved another exciting mystery," Velma says.

"Excuse me," Shaggy says. "But there's still one mystery left to solve."

"What's that?" asks Daphne.

"Like, the mystery of how to convince the cooks here to make Scooby and me some pizza soup!"

Everyone starts laughing.

"Rooby-rooby-roo!" Scooby barks happily.